HUMPERDINK
OUR ELEPHANT FRIEND

For Renata and David, who scatter seeds of play! – S.T.

For Mia, Molly, Eric and Dolores. – C.A.

First published in 2019 by words & pictures,
an imprint of The Quarto Group.
The Old Brewery, 6 Blundell Street,
London N7 9BH, United Kingdom.
T (0)20 7700 6700 F (0)20 7700 8066
www.QuartoKnows.com

A catalogue record for this book is available from the British Library.

ISBN 978 1 78603 542 4

Manufactured in Shenzhen, China PP032019

9 8 7 6 5 4 3 2 1

MIX
Paper from responsible sources
FSC® C001701
www.fsc.org

HUMPERDINK
OUR ELEPHANT FRIEND

words & pictures

At the playgroup I go to,
everyone likes different things.

But the best game we all love is...

...sliding down our slide into

THE BIG CUSHIONS!

Then, one morning, someone new arrived.

Humperdink is an elephant.

He didn't look as if he should be in a playgroup.
He looked as if he should be in a big jungle.

But he came straight in.
And he looked around in such a happy way,
that everyone wanted him to play the things we like.

Ryan got Humperdink to do dressing-up.

But the costumes were a bit too small for an elephant.

A ... A ...

ACHOOOOO!

And Humperdink's big bottom squashed Ryan's favourite hat.

Macey and Kamrul wanted
Humperdink to play hairdressers.

But his head was hard to reach.
And also, he didn't have any hair.

Then I said,
"Let's play hide-and-seek!"

That *seemed* a better idea.

But Humperdink must have
been the worst at hiding
in the whole of the world!

And when some of us did sliding into the big cushions, nobody was thinking Humperdink should try *that*.

But he did.

And our slide...

...BROKE!

Everyone was very sad about the slide.

Humperdink was, too.

And I felt sad for him.

He wasn't trying to be mean.
He was just trying to be
our elephant friend.

So I said, "Maybe we can play the sort of thing YOU like, Humperdink?"

He understood that.

Because he lifted his head.
Then he started elephant-walking.

And elephant-walking looked so fun,
some of us started to follow.

He led us round and round... then outside.

It was sunny!

Humperdink looked so pleased that we were
following, he changed the elephant-walking
to ELEPHANT-STOMPING!

We stumped, stomped and stamped.

But Humperdink suddenly stopped!
He listened! He sniffed like something
DANGEROUS was near!

And he made a sign
for us to climb on his back.

It was as if we were in an actual big jungle!
We all held tight as Humperdink carried us carefully on.

Then we did JUNGLE CLIMBING...

JUNGLE SWINGING...

and JUNGLE JUMPING!

Now, Humperdink *does* know
how to play some things we like.

But the best game we all love
is elephant-walking outside.

And we don't slide down our slide
into the big cushions any more.

We slide down our friend's trunk
into **THE BIG JUNGLE!**